STAR DAMAGE FANTASY GAMEBOOKS PRESENTS

VENGEANCE

A STORY OF REVENGE WHERE YOU PLAY THE HERO!

CHRIS CHILLINGWORTH

VENGEANCE

———

After witnessing the brutal murder of the love of your life to the hands of a facially disfigured killer, you awaken in the hospital determined to find him and kill him.

YOU must take up the challenge and find the killer using persuasion tactics, bribery or violence.

Two dice, a pencil and an eraser, are all you need to embark on this thrilling adventure of revenge and payback. Complete with its elaborate combat system and score sheet to record your gains and losses which change as you progress through the story.

With 17 different endings, you choose the path your character takes on your quest for VENGEANCE.

HOW TO PLAY

Before embarking on your adventure, you must first determine your strengths and weaknesses. You start the story with nothing in your possession.

You must use the dice to determine your initial ATTACK, WOUND and SNEAK scores.

On pages 8-9, there is a Player Sheet which you may use to record the details of your adventure. On it, you will find boxes for recording your ATTACK, WOUND and SNEAK scores.

We recommend recording your scores in pencil, or make photocopies of the page so that you can replay the game whenever you like.

ATTACK, WOUNDS & SNEAK

Roll **one** die. Add +3 to this number and enter this total in the ATTACK box on the Player Sheet.

Roll **both** dice. Add +6 to this number rolled and enter this total in the WOUNDS box.

There is also a SNEAK box. Roll **one** die, add this number and enter the total in the SNEAK box.

ATTACK, WOUNDS and SNEAK scores will change throughout the story. You must keep an accurate record of these scores.

Your ATTACK determines your characters natural ability to fight, useful in any encounters.

Your WOUNDS determines how long you can last and how many wounds you can sustain before you effectively collapse.

Your SNEAK determines your ability to remain undetected.

COMBAT

At various times throughout this story, you may find yourself in a situation where you must fight.

Sometimes the option to SNEAK past a foe may be given, but if not, or if you instead choose to fight, you must resolve the battle as below.

First, any character you encounter and must fight is shown alongside its stats. Such as:-

MONSTER #1
ATT 4
WND 3

The sequence of combat then follows:

1) Roll both dice for the character you are fighting. Add it's ATTACK score. This is their total attack strength.

2) Roll both dice for yourself. Add the number rolled to

your ATTACK score. This is your total attack strength.

3) If your ATTACK strength is higher than your opponent's ATTACK strength, you have wounded your opponent. If your opponents ATTACK strength is higher, then it has instead wounded you. If both scores are the same, you have both avoided wounds this round. Begin again at 1.

4) If you have wounded your opponent, subtract 1 from their WOUNDS score. If your opponent as wounded you, subtract 1 from your WOUNDS score.

5) Begin the next attack round repeating steps 1-4.

Combat ends when either you or your opponent reaches zero WOUNDS. If your WOUNDS score reaches zero, you have lost the combat. If the opponent's WOUNDS score reaches zero, you have won the combat.

Winning combat can have various repercussions and consequences throughout the story.

SNEAK

There are occasions when you may be able to utilise your SNEAK ability, often to avoid combat or conflict.

Should you wish to try, you will be asked to TEST YOUR SNEAK.

Testing your SNEAK is carried out by rolling one die.

Once rolled, compare this number to your current SNEAK score. If the rolled number is equal or lower than your SNEAK score, you pass the test, and the SNEAK is successful. If the rolled number is higher than your SNEAK score, you have lost.

 As a result, raising your SNEAK score throughout the story will increase your chances of rolling under your score and passing tests more often.

WEAPONS

At times during the story, you will have options to pick up certain items such as weapons.

You may only hold one weapon at a time. If you pick up a weapon during the story and are already carrying an item, you must drop that item.

Every weapon in the game comes with it's own ATTACK score boost.

For example, carrying a Hammer might grant you a +2 attack during combat.

Add the +2 bonus to your ATTACK score before your combat begins. This applies to every round of the combat, making it much easier to defeat your foes.

MONEY & BRIBES

There are opportunities throughout the story to BRIBE characters for information.

If this is available, you will be given an option to do so. Choosing to attempt a BRIBE will, in many cases, alter the outcome of the interaction with a character and could avoid combat altogether.

However, to make the BRIBE, you must hold the amount necessary to complete it. If a BRIBE will cost you £500 and you are only carrying £400, you cannot choose that option.

Throughout the story, the amount of MONEY you hold will go up and down. Every time you spend or gain MONEY, you must update it on your player sheet to keep an accurate record of what you have in your possession.

PLAYER SHEET

ATTACK	WOUNDS	SNEAK

MONEY

WEAPON

ADDITIONAL NOTES

COMBAT ENCOUNTERS

ATT WND	ATT WND	ATT WND
ATT WND	ATT WND	ATT WND
ATT WND	ATT WND	ATT WND
ATT WND	ATT WND	ATT WND

TURN OVER TO BEGIN.....

1

———

"FUCK YOU LEON YOU FREAK, LEAVE HIM ALONE!" she screams.

The tension snaps. You feel it, like a change in the air. Perhaps it was the expression on Leon's face changing ever so slightly at the sound of that word she used. "Freak".

It all happened so fast as if your eyes saw it, but your brain couldn't comprehend it. He suddenly had a knife in his hand. You watched the blade as he buried it into her stomach. He did it again. And again. And again.

It was surreal, as if you were watching from afar. Disconnected somehow from the reality of what was taking place. You felt like you were there, but also someplace else. You remember the eerie sense you felt when you realised everyone had been silent the whole time. No screams. Just the wet thuds of the knife slicing into her body. There was so much blood.

And then it hits you smack in the face.

HE STABBED HER!

You race to her. Hold her in your arms. The love of your life looks up at you with an almost vacant expression. The look in her eyes is unrecognisable to you. It is as if she isn't really behind them anymore.

She tries to talk, but she can't. There is blood

everywhere, all over both of you. She is pooling out onto the floor, slipping out of your arms because of it.

"WHAT HAVE YOU D…."

You don't get a chance to finish. A cold icy pain on the back of your head stops you. You've never felt pain like it. You collapse to the ground in shock.

You hear Leon yelling at the barman, the only other person who was there with you in the bar. He's ordering him to clean this mess up.

Your vision turns to black and white, as Leon leaves the bar. A loud engine start's up outside. From where you lay on the sticky blood-covered floor, you look up to the large front window. As your vision fades away, you see Leon pull away on a black Harley Davidson.

Then you pass out.

Turn to 2

2

BEEP…….BEEP…….BEEP

You wake up in a hospital room. A nurse seems to be checking the various machines to which you seem to be connected.

"Oh, you're awake. How are you feeling?" she asks when she notices your eyes opening.

"Lucy!" You ask. "The baby! Are they ok?"

"I'm sorry, I don't know. You've been out of it for a few days. You took a very nasty hit to the head. I'll ask for the doctor to come and see you, but right now you need to rest".

"NO, I want to see Lucy. Just tell me if she's ok. She was stabbed!"

"You need to try and stay calm. You have stitches in your head, and you don't want to aggravate them. The doctor will come and talk to you very soon".

As she opens the door to leave the room, you catch a glimpse of a police officer sitting outside your room. He begins to talk to the nurse before she shuts the door. You couldn't hear what they were saying.

Your mind goes back to that night.

Who the hell was that guy? 'Leon', she called him. Why was he acting as if he knew her? Like they knew each other. She had never mentioned a Leon before. Ever. You know about her old boyfriends. She had always been open about her past. She never said anything about him.

He had that disfigured face. You'll never forget it until the day you die. It was as if he had been burned badly, maybe years ago. Some of his scalp was missing too.

The emotions come rushing in. You start to well up and cry.

The baby. She had only told you that day, surprising you with the news.

The idea of a child had never crossed your mind before. You were too wrapped up in you two to think of the future. It had been two years since you met, but you were still wrapped up in her. You always had been.

So when she showed you the pregnancy test and the excitement in her eyes, it was a shock.

Then there was the worry. The fear that had plagued you all your life. That you were too chicken to care or protect anyone. You had always worried about not being able to protect her. How would you protect a baby?

"Don't worry" she had said. "The very fact you're concerned shows you'll be a great Dad." You didn't know what she meant by that. But she always made you feel better.

Your life had been a mess until you met her. She set you straight and gave you a purpose. Until then you'd followed the wrong people. Got into lousy debt spirals and given up on life.

Lucy is everything to you.

You hope she is ok.

The thoughts go as soon as they come as you drift off to sleep.

Turn to 3

3

You awaken suddenly as the door to your hospital room opens.

A steely-eyed greying doctor walks into your room with a small smile at you and notices you are awake.

The police officer you saw earlier on follows him in before closing the door behind them.

"Mr Underhill, how are you feeling?" says the doctor while looking at your charts.

"Fine. Where's Lucy? Is she okay?", you answer, despite the pounding headache that feels like no headache you've ever had before.

"Mr Underhill, you've suffered a severe concussion, and we've had to put 22 stitches in the back of your head".

"Where's my girlfriend?" you demand.

The police officer then clears his throat before interjecting.

"Mr Underhill, what do you remember about Saturday night?" he says.

"We were at a bar. This guy, Leon she called him, he stabbed her. Will someone please tell me if she's okay? I need to know."

"Mr Underhill, I'm sorry to be the one to have to
tell you this, but Lucy Palmer died of her injuries on
Saturday night. "

Your stomach sinks as you burst into uncontrollable
tears realising the colossal impact of the news.

You will never see Lucy again.

You think of her lying in your arms in fear. That cold
vacant expression on her face as she slipped away from
you. The very memory brings another wave of tears
and emotion. You are a wreck.

"Is there anyone we can call for you?" says the doctor.

There is no one. Lucy was your only family. The new
family you were about to build together. She was
everything to you.

Despite all the grief, one intense feeling continues to
dominate. A feeling that you cannot seem to shake off.
Through all the pain and loneliness you now feel, that
simple idea continues to grow in your mind.

THIS IS ALL YOUR FAULT.

You feel the anger begin to build within you — anger
at yourself.

You were too weak. Too scared. You knew you couldn't
protect her. You failed her. She chose to be with you,
and you couldn't even save her or protect your baby.

"I'm going to need to ask you a few questions about what happened, but I'll give you and few minutes to digest the news Mr Underhill" the officer adds before both men leave the room and close the door behind them.

They'll want to know about Leon. They'll try to find him, arrest him and put him in prison.

It seems unjust. Leon should die for what he's done to you. He doesn't deserve a cell with a bed and 3 square meals a day.

He should die a slow and painful death. The anger within you continues to grow. It's not right. Lucy should be here and he shouldn't.

You've already decided that Leon needs to be punished. You don't trust the police to do it the way it should be.

Plagued with the idea that you failed Lucy and you unborn child you feel determined to seek vengeance. You want Leon to suffer the darkest of sufferings. You want to see him beg for his life and then take it away from him. You are filled with rage. The darkest anger you've ever felt.
You have no one left in this world — no other reason to keep living.

Your only purpose in life now?

To finally stand up and do what you couldn't do when Lucy was alive. To do the right thing and bring real justice down onto that disfigured scumbag.

You're going to kill Leon. **Turn to 4**

4

___

It is night, and the rain is lashing down against the window of your hospital room. It has been several hours since the doctor and officer last came in to check on you. You do not think the police officer likes you. Those looks of disapproval. Almost disgust.

You gingerly climb out of bed, grimacing as your head begins to throb even heavier. You gasp from the sharp, momentary pain as you yank the various tubes from within your arm and remove the sensors stuck to your body. The heart rate monitor alarm starts to sound. You instantly notice a cancel button on the screen and hit it. The room returns to silence but for the rain against the window. It's unlikely anyone heard the noise.

Dressed only in a light blue hospital gown with your belongings nowhere to be seen, you open the door slightly to see the police officer slumped in the chair outside your room. He is fast asleep and snoring loudly.

You scan up and down the hall. You can hear the hustle and bustle of the hospital, but there is no one in the hallway. The coast seems clear.

You have a choice to make.

Do you wake the officer up and alert him to your presence? – **Turn to 28**

Or, make a run for it down the hallway and try to find a way out of the hospital? – **Turn to 12**

5

———

"Whiskey," you tell the barman.

He looks nervous. "Oh shit, sorry we don't have any. Want some Vodka?"

"A bar with no whiskey? Are you kidding me?"

"Sorry, got a shipment coming tomorrow. Vodka?"

"Forget it," you say as you decide against the idea of drinking anyway. "Where's Leon?"

"Look, man, I hate Leon. The things he does. The control he has over everything. I want out. I want nothing to do with it all. But if I rat him out, he'll kill me". The barman looks genuinely scared.

"I'll kill him first."

"Hah. Man, I don't know what world you're on, or how hard he must've hit that head of yours, but there's no way you're getting to Leon. He's untouchable".

"Tell me where he is. Let me worry about that."

"I-I can't man. I'd have to run. I have no money. He'd find me. He owns this place, man. He owns loads of places around here."

You stop to think for a moment. This guy knows where he is. He has the information you need. If you don't get it, you may run out of time to find Leon.

You have a choice.

If you have $1000 on you, you can try to bribe the barman into sharing this information with you. $1000 is enough for him to run away from Leon. If you do not have $1000, you MUST fight him.

If you try to fight the barman and try to beat the location out of him, **Turn to 90**

If you bribe the barman $1000 to tell and run, **Turn to 36**

6

———

LAZLO
ATT 5
WND 4

If you win, **Turn to 67**

If you lose, **Turn to 69**

7

———

Upon walking through the door, you see an empty hallway. The two men have moved onto another room.

But wait…..you can hear them talking.

You walk down the hallway. Halfway down the hall is a door on the left. It reads 'STAFF ONLY', and it's from where the voices are coming.

You move closer to the door to listen to the conversation.

Leon is angrily talking to the other guy. The other guy is hardly saying much.

"Why do I even keep you around Lazlo, you fucking idiot!?".

"Sorry boss," says the other in a strange eastern European accent that you struggle to place.

"If I want a job done, I don't expect to have to do it myself. Now he's out of the hospital and tearing up shit all over the place and probably coming here. Make sure the door guy knows he's coming."

"Already done boss," says Lazlo.

"Then get the fuck outta here and run my club. I'll be in the office!"

You hear another door from within close before seeing the handle of the door you are standing next to begin to open. Someone's coming out!

Turn to 31

8

Bound in your chair, you take a deep breathe and scream for your life.

"HEEEEELP MEEEEE". You repeat it over and over as loud as you can in the vain hope that someone may come running.

Unfortunately, you're in the back storage room of a club, playing loud music, in the loud pouring rain, at what must be 2-3 am when no one is around.

This was possibly the worst idea you've had all night.

Lazlo then comes bursting into the room.

"Shut your fucking trap," he says as he slices your throat with a knife. It was so fast; you didn't even see it coming.

The searing stinging pain turns into choking as you feel blood pouring down your front and running down the back of your throat. You can't breathe for you are chocking on your blood. You begin to feel dizzy and pass out from the sudden blood loss. You can't scream anymore. Over several minutes, you slowly die, on your own, in a storage room at the back of Leon's strip club.

It was all for nothing. You have failed her.

9

———

The smoke was too much for you. Coughing and retching amongst the acrid black smoke that now pours into your lungs you are unable to fight.

Leon takes the opportunity to push you across the room. Disorientated in the smoke, you stumble over a flaming body on the floor. Lazlo is already engulfed in flames and as you land upon him your flailing arms which tried to prevent your fall latch onto the corner of a box full of Vodka.

The bottles land on you, smashing on your head and engulfing you in more flame.

The feeling is excruciating. Like pain, you have never felt. You enter an area of your mind filled with pure chaos and craziness. You begin fighting and lashing out, trying to put out the flame that now engulfs your entire body.

You feel your eyes burning away and the skin melting from your bones. You can't make it to the fire escape. It's pointless anyway.

You pass out from the pain and burn alive.

You have failed. So close.

10

Perhaps you can dart into the bushes across the road that you are already moving towards and hope they continue past.

Perform a SNEAK test.

If you PASS, **Turn to 64**

If you FAIL, **Turn to 93**

11

ROLL to TEST YOUR SNEAK

If SUCCESSFUL, **Turn to 89**
If failed, **Turn to 63**

12

—

ROLL to TEST YOUR SNEAK

If SUCCESSFUL, **Turn to 53**
If failed, **Turn to 28**

13

———

The old town is a quaint traditional area of town. An abundance of fish and chip shops and antique bric-a-brac stores line the cobbled streets. The early Tudor style houses of white and black attract tourists by day, but by night the area takes on a much seedier persona.

Frequented by drug users, tramps and criminals, the area is considered a place to avoid at nightfall.

You pull your car up nearby, but the old cobbled streets make it difficult to find a parking space for your vehicle.

You go forwards on foot for a while down the main cobbled street towards the poker house.

Perhaps it's the weather tonight, but the place seems deathly quiet. A stray dog scurries through a fallen bin, looking for scraps in the rain.

Eventually, you reach the poker club. It would have been easy to miss. A small inconspicuous black door that opens onto the street seems to be the only way inside. It's locked, however, and you notice an intercom buzzer on the wall beside it.

You can't buzz it. You were hoping for a less visible entrance. "Hi, I'm here to kill Leon" probably won't get you in.

Just then, you hear talking. Someone is coming out.

The door begins to open in front of you.

ROLL to TEST YOUR SNEAK

If SUCCESSFUL, **Turn to 91**
If failed, **Turn** to 85

14

———

You head to the front of the building. You don't have long before the guy in the office will raise the alarm. You clear your throat as you approach to alert the man of your presence.

The tall man in the black coat drops the box he's carrying and turns around to face you.

"WHO'S THERE?" he says in alarm.

"Hey," you say, stepping forward into the light. "I'm looking for Leon, have you seen him?".

The guy says nothing for a moment. You're about to fill the awkward silence when he takes a step closer, leans in and asks "Hey, are you the guy?".

"The guy?" you ask, uncertain of what he means.

"Yeah, the guy with the dead wife," he says, looking over his shoulder and being sure to keep his voice down.

The nonchalant nature of how he addressed Lucy pisses you off. You envisage beating this guys head in just for saying those words.

You don't realise it, lost in your anger, but your eyes are looking through your eyebrows. Covered in blood, standing in the rain, you probably look a little psychopathic. "where the fuck is Leon?" you repeat.

The guy takes a step closer, once again taking a look over his shoulder to check no one is listening.

"Hey man, chill. Listen, I'm going to help you. Leon's not here. But I know where he is tonight."

"Where"? You ask. Wanting to see if he would corroborate the story you've just been told by the guy upstairs.

The guy lowers his voice more, but loud enough that you can hear over the rain.

"He's at Scarlett's. It's a strip joint down at the seafront opposite the pier. It's closed, but it's open if you catch me. Police down here let him do what he wants. He owns the whole place. He'll be down there all night. Always is."

"I was told he was in here and the guy upstairs says he's at the poker house. Now you say he's at a strip joint. Are you messing with me?" you say as you maintain eye contact the whole time.

"Nah man, you don't want to go there. Listen, I promise you, he's not here. I know he's at Scarlett's tonight. Trust me".

"Why do you want to help me?" you ask, surprised at the apparent level of treason seemingly being committed by one of Leon's staff.

"Dude, fuck Leon. He controls everything and everyone. I'm sick of it. He does what he wants and never pays for it. Last week he smacked my girl around the face for nothing but his temper. She's got a broken fucking nose. There's nothing I can do about it if I want to live. The sooner he gets a kicking from someone the better. Guy thinks he's untouchable. But man let me tell you, if you mess with him, make sure you finish the job. You don't want a man like Leon chasing you. You'll be running for a lifetime. And don't tell him I told you any of this. He'll kill me."

You like this kid. Either he's a fantastic liar, or he's telling the truth. His words, emotions and expressions seem genuine.

"Thanks for the advice" you say, as you turn and walk off back to your car.

If you head to the Poker House, **Turn to 13**

If instead, you decide to go to Scarlett's, **Turn to 66**

15

———

You struggle in his grip, but your feet are off the ground. You have no leverage from which to fight. You swing your arms and legs, but you're unable to land any sharp blows.

You feel your neck crushing and the life force being taken from you. Your sight begins to go black and white, and you feel a dizziness before everything goes black.

You wonder if you're dead. Then you realised if you were, you probably wouldn't be wondering if you were dead.

At that very moment, a cold icy splash of water hits your face and upper body. You awaken with panic and gasp at the coldness of the water.

As you shake the water off, you find yourself in a dark room with no windows. The tiled floor and walls are crumbling. It feels like you may be underground. A basement perhaps?

You hear female whimpering noises from all around you. As you look around, you are horrified to see several skeletal women handcuffed and tied to railings cemented into the walls.

You are inside an underground prison of some kind. Blood and faeces have been smeared across the floor.

The room reeks of death, rot and putrid human waste making you gag.

Then you see him standing in front of you. He is wearing a sharp navy blue suit with slick wet-look hair and a stubbled chin. He is tall, and slender with an athletic build with eastern European features to his face. He looks oddly out of place in a room like this.

He begins to speak in an odd accent you cannot place.

"You see this knife?" he asks, wielding it before you both? "You recognise it?". "You've probably seen it before".

LUCY! He's holding the knife that Leon had that night.

You struggle to get up, but you are strapped to a chair and strapped well. Even the chair itself will not seem to budge. You try to speak, but you are gagged and can only make a noise.

He laughs out loud before walking towards you, still wielding the knife.

"You ignorant fool. Thinking you can come here and do what? Attack us in our fortress? I admire your courage and determination. You have created quite the stir tonight. But it was all for nothing, my friend."

And with a bolt of rage, he slices your neck, slowly, with the knife.

The searing stinging pain turns into choking as you feel blood pouring down your front and running down the back of your throat. You can't breathe, and you begin to feel dizzy. You pass out from the sudden blood loss and over several minutes, slowly die to the sound of starving dying women crying.

You have failed her.

16

____

As you open the green door, you immediately notice
a set of stairs leading down. About halfway down the
stairs, you meet with a putrid smell of human waste,
rot and decay.

The very smell causes you to gag and retch
involuntarily. It is a vile stench that offends every sense
you have.

As you reach the bottom of the stairs, you find another
doorway. Opening this doorway, you realise where the
stench is coming from.

You enter a basement. The old decaying tiles that
line the floor are stained in old blood and what looks
and smells like human excrement. The walls are
crumbling and are in a terrible state of disrepair. The
walls themselves have what seem to be iron railings
cemented into them that run the perimeter of the
whole room.

Chained to these railings, approximately 20 women,
all naked and skeletal in appearance. Some have died;
most are almost dead. 1 or 2 are moaning quietly. They
are being starved to death down here.

The very sight of this causes you to vomit on the floor.

You do not hear the footsteps behind you. You only feel
the icy sting of a blade sliding into your back before

being taken out. Repeated, this time higher up between your ribs. Again, another blade slides into your body as it goes into shock.

You fall to your knees and collapse on the floor.

You never saw your killer as the room went black. You die of your wounds within minutes, accompanied by the sounds of footsteps leaving the room and dying women whimpering in the distance.

You failed.

17

———

You awaken, handcuffed to a chair in a back room surrounded with boxes on shelves. It looks like a storage room full of alcohol for the club. On the other side of the room is a fire escape. It seems like it probably leads outside. Perhaps the rear door you saw from the car park.

You notice all your things laid out on the desk. They have taken them while you were out cold.

LOSE ALL YOUR ITEMS YOU WERE CARRYING FROM YOUR PLAYER SHEET.

Leon is standing by the table, inspecting your stuff when he notices you coming round.

"Ah, the warrior awakens". He laughs before looking you in the eye and taking out the knife that you recognised earlier.

"Remember this?" he says. Lazlo gave you a nasty gash with it, but I used it to do far more.

"You'll won't live to see the morning" you answer. Blood running from your nose. Every inch of your body aching in pain from the trials of the night.

Leon bursts out in laughter. "And you think you'll be the one to end my life, eh? Tough talk from a man handcuffed to a chair in my office."

You try to pull your hand through the handcuffs to break free. They're not on tight, but tight enough that you can't get your hand through.

"Funny how some people never know when they're beaten. Fascinating that despite already failing, you still keep fighting."

"Why," you ask. "Why did you do it?"

Leon smirks and then begins to pace around the room, playing with the knife in his hands while he talks.

"My friend, I know that you've taken a blow to the head. But are you that dense?"

"You knew her?" you ask.

Leon smiles. "It was a bit more than that," he says, laughing.

"What did she ever do to you?"

Leon erupts into a rage. "What did she do? WHAT DID SHE FUCKING DO????". He reaches down, grabs your top and pulls you close, face to face. His disfigured burned face is breathing into yours as you see with detail the scars and blistered skin covering his features. He points to his face.

"THIS! THIS is what she did to me."

You look at him in disbelief. The woman you know wouldn't have inflicted such an injury on someone for no reason.

"What did you do to her?"

Leon's demeanour violently flips from calm to rage and back to calm. It is as if he cannot control it.

"Ok, ok. I may have been a bit rough." He says smiling with a jokey tone, but erupting again into a rage "But that is NO fucking excuse for what she did. Burning my face in the fucking fire."

"I fucking hate fire. I should have killed her long ago." He adds calmly. "In truth, she should never have come back. Fancy meeting her in the bar that night. Who did she think she was, coming back to my town, after what she did".

You look at him. Envisaging what you would do if you got your hands on him.

"Anyway, it's been nice to meet you. He says with a chuckle. "My buddy Lazlo is going to be popping by again to see you. Wants to finish the job. I've asked him not to make too much mess in here. Don't want to damage the stock, do we?" he says, laughing away to himself as he leaves the room through the door you must have come in from.

The moment he leaves the room, you frantically begin to try and break free of the chair. You can hear more talking from a distance. It sounds like Lazlo again.

You will die here unless you can find a way out of here.

You look down at your feet. They are tied with string. It would be easy to break free if you had your hands.

You try to slip your hands through the cuffs again, but they are just tight enough to prevent it.

You look around the room for an answer but find nothing.

You can scream for help and hope that someone hears you. It's a long shot, but you're in trouble here and running out of options.

Or, you can force your hands out of the handcuffs. It'll hurt like hell, but a pair of broken thumbs or wrists is nothing if it means you get free.

What will you do?

If you scream for help, **Turn to 8**

If you try to break free of the handcuffs, **Turn to 51**

18

___

The blow to the head you delivered to Leon does not kill him. It only stuns him for a moment. Despite that, blood is running from his head down into his eyes. As he comes around again, surrounded in flames, he struggles to wipe the blood from his eyes to see.

He begins to walk towards the fire, trying to find the door to get out as he frantically wipes more blood out of his eyes. His head wound is delivering more blood, faster than he can get rid of it.

He eventually finds the door, but you had already closed it behind you when you left the room. He sees you through the reinforced window of the door.

You use your body weight and your wounded hand to try and stop him from turning the handle. His face is sheer panic, and he is screaming in fear.

Your heart is pounding in your chest as you wonder to yourself if you have enough strength to keep the door closed while you try to lock it

You frantically rummage through the keys you took off Lazlo trying to find the key that looked like it fit. It's hard to do with one hand.

There! You found it! You insert it into the lock and twist. The lock slides into place. You leave the key lodged in the keyhole and watch Leon from the window.

Half the room is now engulfed in flames, and you begin to hear bottles exploding and flames shooting across the room. Leon's screams are blood curdling as he frantically tries to break the window with his fists. The reinforced glass is taking no apparent damage.

A look then appears over Leon's face. You would describe it as happiness or relief, perhaps.

He runs over to the fire escape on the other side of the room, not yet engulfed in flames.

He tries to push the door open, but it won't budge. He tries again, without luck. He begins to cry out again in panic.

"NO, NOT LIKE THIS!!!!" he screams as he looks at the flames starting to light parts of his clothing.

It must be so hot in there. You can no longer stand close to the door; the heat must be unbearable inside.

Desperately Leon steps back and takes a run-up to the fire escape. He launches himself at it in a bid to make it move. The door remains closed.

Of course, he cannot open it; his bike is propped up against it.

Before you came in through the front door of the club, you placed his motorbike against the door, using his security chain and the nearby dumpsters for added effect. It'll take an army to break that door open.

Leon looks at you, in agony, knowing what you have done. The flames are now riding up his trousers and almost reaching his waist.

He looks at you with a shocked stare, you recognise very well.

"That's for Lucy," you say to him, as you leave the room back into the hallway.

As you make your way back into the main club room, you realise that no one seems to have noticed that half the building is now on fire. Punters are still throwing money at the girl on stage. You glance over at the barman. He's too busy dealing with a man vomiting onto the bar to notice you walking through the room.

The fire alarm triggers as you reach the main exit. Sending half-clothed dancers and miserable old punters to scurry to the front door with you as you leave.

You flood out into the car park, amid a panic-stricken and confused crowd.

Suddenly an explosion rips through the back of the club, sending flames billowing out from the back door. The crowd gasp and instinctively crouch down in shock. Leon's bike is sent across the other side of the alleyway as the fire exit door is blown open. Flames are pouring from the room you were just inside.

The room is entirely engulfed in flame. You can no longer hear Leon's screams.

As the various fire engines begin to arrive at the scene, you notice the rain has finally stopped. You walk away from the commotion, nursing your leg and hand into the dark early morning of the next day unnoticed amid the chaos you leave behind.

You may not have been able to help her. She may no longer be here. But for once in your sorry life, you've done the one thing you've never dared to do.

Stand up and fight. And you'll fight now until the end of your days.

Turn to 100

19

———

You've been at the poker table now for what feels like about 30 minutes and played a few hands.

One of the men called the cigar man Eddie earlier. Eddie has been mopping up the table and has a huge chip stack as well as a set of car keys and some jewellery that other players have seemingly lost throughout the night.

You are running out of money, and you're not going to last much longer.

Eddie catches you looking at the keys and jewellery next to his chip stack.

"One thing about me, you should know. You don't get to owe me. I don't have time to chase debts. You pay now, or I take what I want". He says.

"And what if I don't have anything to give?" you ask.

"Then we all spend the evening making you wish you never set foot in here".

"So how do I get out of here alive?" you ask.

Eddie laughs and looks around at the table.

"Easy," he says, "you win a hand".

"One hand?" you ask.

"Sure, why not. Feeling generous." He says as he looks you in the eye.

"That, and I've been winning all fucking night!" he explodes with laughter. The rest of the table smile but they are all intimidated by this Eddie guy. They laugh at every joke in fear of pissing him off.

Eddie is playing aggressively, going all-in on almost every hand. You are going to have to go all-in to try and survive against him.

You calculate in your head that you'll need to go all-in on one of the next four hands you have.

You have a decision to make.

Which hand are you going to go all-in on?

On this hand, you are dealt a KC & 10C.

If you go all in here, **Turn to 27.**

If you play another hand, **Turn to 94.**

20

————

Gregor is far too strong for you. The first blow he landed on you felt like being hit by a truck. Lying on the floor, you felt the bones in your arm shatter as you instinctively tried to protect yourself from the subsequent blows that followed.

Then he was on top of you. Blow after blow, the metal of the spanner smashing into your face. You felt your facial bones shatter and break under the immense pressure and saw blood splattering across his face. It wasn't his.

You wake up struggling to be able to see. You are in so much pain. Like nothing, you have felt before. Every inch of you is in searing agony. You outwardly groan in pain. It's all you can manage.

You manage to open one eye. You are in the backseat of a car, your arms crudely tied to your sides with industrial tape. Not that it was necessary. Moving is excruciatingly painful. You can't bring yourself even to try and break the tape.

Then you notice the engine of the car is running. No one is in the driver's seat. The doors are closed, and the driver's window is slightly open with a hose pipe sticking into the car from outside. The gap in the window has been taped up.

The car is smoky and the fumes you are breathing feel

like hot lava burning through your nasal passages and into your lungs.

You choke as your one remaining eye burns, and the tears streaming from them prevent you from seeing anything.

You cry out for it to stop, but it's a desperate cry as you know that no one is coming for you.

As you feel the black toxic chemicals flowing into your lungs, everything drifts away, and you slip into the black.

You failed Lucy again.

21

You are dealt a pair of Aces. AS & AC. You have to go all-in on this hand. So you do.

Turn to 32.

22

———

Your bus journey to town was uneventful. The whole bus was empty. You spent most of the time thinking about Lucy and how you'll kill Leon when you find him. You ring the bell as you notice the bus approaching the stop close to the bar and shout at the driver through the wind and rain to confirm the day and time as you step off.

"Day?" he scoffs, raising his voice to be heard. "It's Tuesday night. 1 am, so technically Wednesday" he replies before closing the bus doors smiling away to himself in disbelief and driving off.

Tuesday night? Lucy died on Saturday night. It's been three days???

The realisation shocks you somewhat, but it makes no difference. You hope Leon is still around. He's a dead man walking.

Turn to 71.

23

———

Following the road and footpath around the tall hospital building, you eventually see the hospital car park. It's quiet, so it's probably quite late. You head on over to it and notice a dedicated bus lane with several bus stops.

You could walk to town from here, but it's a long slog to get home. Too far, especially in this weather. It would easily take an hour. Maybe longer. A bus may be your only option right now.

The bus stop shelters are empty, with no one within. You wipe the rain off the soaking wet laminated timetable board to see when the next bus is coming, but with no way of telling the time you have no idea how long you'll have to wait, or if the busses even run this late. It's also very dark, and there's little in the way of lighting nearby.

Then, as if like magic, the timetable you were intensely scrutinising lights up amid the headlight beams that have flooded the bus stop. Your heart skips a beat as you momentarily wonder if you've been caught.

That is until you realise the sound of the bus headed your way.

It pulls up at the stop. The 711. You know this bus. It heads close to where you live. You could head off home and pick up some supplies. You'll need something to help you find Leon tonight, and then deal with him when you do.

As the bus doors open, you notice another bus pull up behind the 711. The 120. You know this bus too. It's the bus that shuttles from the hospital to the town. You could head straight to the bar and get some information out of that Barman. Maybe break his skull in half while you're at it.

You ask the driver how much the fare is. £5 for an all-night ticket.

You have a decision to make. If you have any cash, you can take one of the busses. If you have no cash, you MUST walk.

If you take the 711 to home, LOSE -£5 from your cash and **Turn to 83.**

If you take the 120 to town, LOSE -£5 from your cash and **Turn to 22.**

If you choose to walk to town, **Turn to 55.**

24

Your stuff is missing, your thumb is broken, and your leg is gashed. You had no hope against this trained killer. He also had a knife. It found it's way into your throat somehow and got stuck there.

The last thing you feel as you lay on the floor is the blade being slid back out of your throat. You've already choked to death on your blood at this point. You die on the floor of Leon's storage room where no one will miss you. No one knows you're even here.

Leon will carry on doing what he wants. This whole quest was all for nothing.

25

——

You walk around to the side of the building, ensuring the guy round the front doesn't notice you. The rain is still lashing down, and there is very little light down the side passage of the building. It is easy to remain undetected.

You look up as you go past the stairs. The light is still on up there, and you press on to make sure you are not spotted.

As you reach the rear of the building, you see a courtyard with another garage across onto the other side. There are cars littered around. Many of them look as if they have been involved in accidents of some kind. Some are stripped down with all their interiors missing.

In the building opposite, you can hear music playing, and you see a light. It sounds like someone is listening to the radio. Above the sound of rain hitting the cars, you can hit someone tinkering and the sounds of spanners being dropped and something being hit.

There is someone over there.

Using the cars and the darkness as cover, you move in closer.

You can see someone in there that resembles a large-framed man in grey overalls. He's working on a car and seemingly ripping out the interior seats. It's not Leon, but he might know where Leon is.

You have a choice to make.

If you speak to this man and ask him where Leon is, turn to 57.

If you change your mind and decide to go and speak to the man out the front, turn to 46.

If you decide to instead to and investigate the offices upstairs, turn to 95.

26

You are dealt a pair, KD & KH. Its either this hand or the next that you have to go all in on?

If you go all in here, **Turn to 61**

If you play another hand, **Turn to 21**

———

27

You go all-in, and all other players except Eddie fold. Eddie calls your bet.

You lay down your cards face-up on the table, a KC and 10C. Eddie chuckles as he then lays his cards down, staring at you from across the table with a grin on his face.

An AS and a 10D

You'll only win this is you get a King.

The cards come down. An 8D, a 3D, and a JD. Eddie is on for a flush draw, and you have nothing.

The next card comes down. A 2C. It helps neither player.

Finally, the last card is flipped.

An AD.

Eddie not only has a pair of aces but a flush draw with 5x diamonds.

You lose.

Eddie takes your chips while laughing. You gulp at the very idea of taking on six men in a fight.

"Get lost," he says. "SCRAM!".

"I can go?".

Eddie gets up from the table and walks over to the bar. He picks up a whiskey and pours himself a drink.

"I can't be bothered today. I already got your money. But if I see you around here again, I will have Michail cut your face off." He says, nodding towards the large fellow sitting at the other end of the table.

You get up without your money and walk out of the poker room via the door you came in from.

DEDUCT ALL Cash from your Cash on your Player Sheet

Turn to 68.

28

The overweight officer suddenly wakes up from his slumber. Alarmed, embarrassed and frightened to see you out of your bed, the officer panics. He jumps up from his seat and grabs his stick out from his tool belt.

You hold your hands out before you and shout "no, no it's fine, please", but the officer is taken over by a mixture of fear and confusion. You can see it in his eyes.

You back away realising that waking him was a mistake, backwards into the same room you were trying to leave. He follows and begins wildly swinging at you with his stick.

You have no choice; you must fight him to continue with your mission to kill Leon.

CUMBERSOME POLICE OFFICER
ATT 3
WND 3

If you win, **Turn to 43**
If you lose, **Turn to 34**

29

———

You instantly punch the barman aiming for his nose.
You miss, hitting him directly in the throat instead.
He falls to the ground, choking, struggling to breathe.
Holding his hands up in surrender as you climb over
the bar to finish him off.

"He's at Trevors, the car shop! Russell Street, by the
cinema! Just don't kill me!!!!" he pleads.

"Trevors?" you ask.

"He owns it; he's there most nights with his crew.
Please don't kill me!"

You back down, allowing him to live. You're not going
to kill a man begging for his life.

You head to the door, taking one last look at the blood-
stained floor where she died before venturing back out
into the wind and rain.

You're going to Trevors.

Turn to 73.

30

How you beat such a monster you have no idea. Somehow your rage, coupled with a couple of lucky dodges and one lucky blow to his head managed to knock the guy down. Once he was down, the rest was relatively easy.

He won't be getting up again. Ever.

You suddenly panic. Were you heard? The rain, the music, the banging of ripping out seats. Was it enough to cover the sound of the struggle?

It didn't last long, and no one has come running. If there was anyone in the office, they probably couldn't hear.

You won't be getting any information from this guy now. Although you know you're in the right place.

You have another decision to make.

If you visit the office and see who's up there, **Turn to 95.**

If you go around the front of the building and speak to the guy unloading the truck, **Turn to 46.**

31

The door opens, and you quickly move to the side. The tall suited man you saw earlier in the main club room leaves the room and closes the door behind him without looking. He begins to walk in the opposite direction from you when he hears you. He turns around in surprise to see you standing right there in the hallway.

You must fight him.

LAZLO
ATT 5
WND 4

If you win, **Turn to 76.**

If you lose, **Turn to 82.**

———

You go all-in, and all other players except Eddie fold. Eddie calls your bet.

You lay down your cards face-up on the table. Pocket rockets! You have a pair of aces AS and an AC. Eddie looks at you as he then lays his cards down, staring you down from across the table.

He lays a KD and a 6H. It's a weak hand, especially against yours.

The cards come down. 4C, AD and 5D. Eddie has a chance at a 5x diamond flush, but it's weak. You have 3x Aces already. It's a strong position.

Eddie is looking angry.

The next card comes down — a KS. Eddie has 2x Kings, but it doesn't beat your Aces.

Finally, the last card is flipped down onto the table.

8H! It does nothing for either player, so you win with a pair of Aces. The perfect hand to go all-in on! Well done!

 You gulp at the very idea of taking on six men in a fight, however.

"Get lost" Eddie shouts. "SCRAM!".

"I can go?".

Eddie gets up from the table and walks over to the bar. He picks up a whiskey and pours himself a drink.

"If I see you around here again, I will have Michail cut your face off." He says, nodding towards the large fellow sitting at the other end of the table.

You get up with your money and walk out of the poker room via the door you came in.

TRIPLE the amount of MONEY you are currently carrying and UPDATE your Cash on your player Cash sheet.

Turn to 68.

33

ROLL to TEST YOUR SNEAK

If SUCCESSFUL, **Turn to 65**
If failed, **Turn to 52.**

34

———

The Police Officer cracks you over the head with his baton. Your sight fades to black and white, and you feel blood dripping down your face as everything goes black.

You wake up hours later in a police cell. Your head is throbbing harder than ever. The officer is sitting outside the cell, looking in at you through the bars. He chuckles to himself.

"I always knew you did it — you sick psycho. You'll rot in here".

That's why he didn't like you. He thinks you did it!

Nevertheless, you'll struggle to convince him and everyone else now. Leon will have the barman on his side no doubt. There'll be a lengthy court battle, and you may not ever get your vengeance on Leon after all.

You failed her….again.

It's over before it even got started.

35

______

It's warm inside. And dry. A welcome change to standing out in the cold rain all night. You enter into a long narrow hallway. A table of various dripping wet coats lay on the table near the door, with many hanging up on hooks as well.

There is nothing else in the hallway apart from the well-trodden grey carpet you walk on and a very dimly lit bulb that provides just enough light to allow you to see where you are going.

At the end of the narrow hallway is a door.

You walk down the hallway to the door and open it.

Inside, you find a small room which looks like it may have once been a kitchen. The dirty filthy room is just about big enough to fit a fridge with a TV on top of it, and a small table and chairs. On the other side of the room to your left is another door. A large framed, slightly overweight man is sitting with his feet are up on the table rocking back in his chair while watching a TV. He turns around to look at you with a puzzled look on his face.

He has a disturbingly deep voice. "Who are you?" he asks.

"I'm here to play cards" you answer, assuming that lying would be the best way to get into the back room and find Leon.

"You're not a member here, I've never seen you before. How did you get in?" he asks as he gets out of his chair. His massive 6ft frame is filling the room and now blocking your sight of the TV.

You can try to fight this guy, but he seems strong and maybe beyond you. He doesn't strike you as a man with a lot of money, however, and you only want to go into the back room. Every man wants something. Persuasion is about working out what someone else wants so you can get what you want.

You have a choice to make.

If you have the money, you may try to bribe the doorman $500. If you cannot afford it, however, then you must try to fight him.

If you attempt to bribe the doorman, **Turn to 40.**

If you fight the doorman, **Turn to 81.**

36

———

LOSE -$1000 from the cash section of your player sheet.

"Listen, I get it" you explain as you take out your cash. "Here's the deal. I will give you $1000 cash right now if you tell me where he is. I won't tell him that you told me, and he'll be dead by morning anyway once I get my hands on him. You can turn and run. That's enough money to get the hell out of this town. You change even your name and leave this all behind. Whaddya say?"

The barman's look is serious. He is genuinely thinking about your proposal.

"Fine" he eventually says, taking your cash from you. "I wanted out of this place anyway". "Go to Trevors Motors the Car Shop on Russell Street. Just down from the cinema. Use the back door to get in. No one goes in the front. It's not that far from here. You'll find him there with his fucking dogs around him, man. Be warned. He's untouchable. He'll have you killed, man."

"Sure," you say as you leave the bar. You steal a glance over your shoulder at Lucy's blood on the floor, then look at the barman, before you walk out of there, never to set foot in there again.

Turn to 73.

37

———

He doesn't have time to react. You reacted faster. You grab a heavy bottle of Vodka from the shelf beside you and smash it over his head. The blow lands right on his temple, and he collapses to the ground.

He's out. Cold. Blood running from the side of his head.

You rummage through his expensive suit jacket to find a box of cigarettes and 2x disposable lighters in his inside pocket. In his trousers, you find a handkerchief and a box of matches. You also take his keys off his belt. There are four keys on the ring; one looks like it may belong to the door of the room.

Moving as fast as you can with one hand you break open the lighters and pour the fluid inside onto the handkerchief. It goes up quickly with the accelerant. You throw the flaming handkerchief onto the cardboard boxes that line the shelves and pour the remaining liquid over the now spreading flames — tossing in the box of matches for added effect.

The boxes burst into flames. The alcohol inside likely to break under the heat soon and add more fuel.

The fire becomes well established, and the room fills quickly with acrid black smoke that makes it hard to breathe. You find a pair of worker gloves on the floor and use them crudely to put over your nose and mouth. You need to stay in there for another few seconds.

Then the opportunity arises.

Leon bursts into the room. "WHAT THE...." he shouts in alarm. He doesn't have time to finish as he doubles over and begins hacking up the black smoke he took deep into his lungs.

By now, the room is full of smoke.

From where you are crouching down beside the wall, you can see Leon and the doorway. He is well into the room now, seemingly trying to find you and Lazlo. You notice how close he is to stumbling upon Lazlo's unconscious body.

You have a choice to make. It may be the most critical choice you have made all night.

Do you take this moment to fight Leon? Or you can sneak past him and try to lock him in the room using the keys you took off Lazlo?

If you fight Leon in the smoke-filled room full of alcohol, **Turn to 42.**

If instead, you try to sneak past Leon amid the smoke-filled room and try to lock him in, **Turn to 33.**

38

REMOVE -£2000 from your cash on your Player Sheet

"Wait….wait!" You shout as he storms towards you, fists clenched. "I want to speak to Leon. Let me in, and I'll make it worth your while. £2000? I have it on me right now. Just let me in there, and we'll say I slipped past you?".

He smacks away the cash that you were waving at him, scattering the notes across the street in the wind and rain. He grabs you by the throat and lifts you off your feet. You weren't ready for this.

The Doorman isn't interested in the money.

You must fight your way out of this mess.

Turn to 88.

39

———

You're not sure how you did it, but once again, you've excelled yourself. That's the thought that goes through your head anyway while you stand over the groaning body of the doorman. Lying in the cobbled street outside the poker house, in the pouring torrential rain, he is……sobbing?

Yes, he is crying.

"I'm sorry, he says. Please don't hurt me anymore. I was just doing my job" he moans, clutching his leg.

"Leon? Where is he?" you demand, standing over him.

"He's not here. He's at the strip club. Scarlett's. He's always there."

You turn and walk away in the rain.

"He knows you're coming!" shouts the doorman as you walk away back towards where you parked the car.

"Good" you reply.

Turn to 58.

40

DEDUCT -$500 from your cash on your Player Sheet

"Listen," you say to the giant standing before you. "What if I gave you $400? I have it with me now; all I want is to get inside. I won't cause any trouble".

The doorman thinks about it for a second before replying.

"$500 and if anyone asks you, you tell them those other two idiots let you in, not me." He finally says.

"Agreed," you say as you count the money and hand it over. Glad to not have to try and fight this monstrosity of a man.

He pockets the cash and sits back down at the table to watch TV as if he hasn't seen you.

You go on into the room.

Turn to 44

41

___

Holding him against the wall by his throat, you can see the life slipping away from him. His eyes are turning from panic to acceptance of the end.

It was close; he almost got the knife he had been reaching for. With both hands around his neck, you would have been an open target if he reached it. But a swift hip twist prevented him from getting there.

You had pictured so many different ways of killing Leon. The romantic in you wanted to burn him alive. But you can't be choosy in times like these. You have to take these opportunities as they're presented to you.

Nevertheless, losing his life to your bare hands round his neck was probably up there in the top 5. It was more personal. Almost as if she were there herself watching him slip away.

He lost consciousness, but you still kept going. To be sure.

Eventually, when you were certain he was no longer breathing, you allowed his body to collapse to the floor, half propped up against the wall.

You take a quick look at the monitors. The kitchen staff are all still chopping what looks like chunks of meat with their machetes. They do not seem to have heard any of the struggles.

Everything looks normal in the club.

You decide, however, that with the job done, you should leave as soon as possible. Meeting a gang of machete-wielding cooks would not end well for you.

You rifle through Leon's pockets and find a small set of keys which you take before leaving the room and venturing out back to the rear exit of the building. You step over Lazlo's dead body as you leave silently and close the fire exit door behind you.

Starting up Leon's bike, the engine sounds incredible. Vibrations of the engine running straight through you as you sit on the padded seat and place your hands on the long extended handlebars.

It's been years since you rode a motorcycle. Not since you were a teenager, but it doesn't take long to come back to you.

Then you notice it. The rain. It's stopped entirely.

Taking a long deep breathe you pull away on Leon's motorcycle, feeling the torque pull you away from the events of tonight. Out into the darkness of what's left of the night.

You have no idea where you're headed. Somewhere new.

You may not have been able to help her. She may no longer be here. But for once in your sorry life, you've done the one thing you'd never previously found the courage to do.

Stand up and fight. And you'll fight now until the end of your days.

Turn to 100.

42

——

You are unable to breathe amid the flames and acrid smoke.

Deduct -2 STR before the start of this fight.

Leon is also struggling to breathe in the fire and suffers a low STR rating as a result.

LEON 'THE FACE'
ATT 3
WND 8

If you win, **Turn to 18.**

If you lose, **Turn to 9.**

43

———

You killed a police officer! You never intended for him to get hurt, but it was a choice between going to prison and failing Lucy yet again, or Leon getting what he deserves. No one, not even the law, will get in your way anymore.

You spend a few minutes shaken. You've never killed anyone before. But you have nothing left to lose in this life. Your hatred for Leon and what he had done to those you love is stronger than the fear of repercussion. More determined than ever, you look out the door to see if the coast is clear. Thankfully, no one seems to have heard the commotion.

Being barefooted helps as you leave the room quietly. You race down the hallway as quietly as you can, taking a glance over your shoulder as you go through the double doors leaving the hall.

You leave the hallway to find busy corridors full of staff and patients all making their way to different areas of the hospital. It's easy to fit in, although it's obvious you're a patient when wearing nothing but a hospital gown.

Turn to 62.

44

———

Upon entering the room, you find a dimly lit, smoky poker room with one table that sits nine players. Six men sit around the table. One is pacing around the room on his mobile phone.

There is a door behind them with the word Toilet on it, and another door which you presume leads out to the rear of the building. Both doors are closed.

The only other thing in the room is a cocktail bar on the far left side with two old bar stools. The bar is stocked full of various alcoholic drinks.

The room was a cacophony of laughter and shouting when you walked in. Now, the whole room is silent. Even the guy on the phone has gone quiet. Every single one of these men is staring at you.

None of them appears friendly.

"I'm looking for Leon," you say.

The men begin to exchange glances with one another.

"How the fuck did you get in?" asks one guy sitting at a table smoking a cigar.

"I just need to talk to Leon".

"Leon ain't fucking here, who are the fuck are you?" says the cigar man.

The guy on the mobile phone has finished his call and walks around behind you, blocking your exit.

You feel the tension in the room.

"I'm just a guy, looking for Leon".

"He's just a guy looking for Leon!" says the cigar man to his mates around the table. They all erupt in laughter.

"Well, Leon ain't fucking here bud, so you're all out of luck" he adds with a lowered and more sinister tone.

"Do you know where he is?" you ask.

"Who the fuck knows where Leon is? He comes and goes when he wants."

"Right. Well, I won't bother you guys any longer." You say before turning to leave. The mobile phone man remains in your way, looking you straight in the eye.

"Not so fast". Says the cigar man. "You can't just walk into this 'ere club, start spouting demands and walk back out again". "You're going to play some cards".

"No thanks, I got somewhere I need to be. Another time." You reply.

The cigar man laughs out loud and snorts.

"This guy still doesn't get it, eh, fellas?". "I'm telling you, you ain't leaving unless you play".

You look around the room. It would be six against one. There's no way you could win this or even get out alive.

You have no choice. You'll have to play.

Turn to 19.

You go all-in, and all other players except Eddie fold. Eddie calls your bet.

You lay down your cards face-up on the table, a KD and an AD. Eddie looks at you as he then lays his cards down, staring at you from across the table.

He places down a 7H and a KS. It's a weak hand.

The cards come down. 7C, 9S and QS. Eddie has a pair of 7's and is on for a weak flush draw, and you have nothing.

The next card comes down. An AD. It puts you on top! You now have a pair of Aces. Eddie loses his chance for a flush.

Finally, the last card is flipped over.

It's another Ace. AC. You win with 3 of the kind Aces!

 You gulp at the very idea of taking on six men in a fight.

"Get lost" he says. "SCRAM!".

"I can go?".

Eddie gets up from the table and walks over to the bar. He picks up a whiskey and pours himself a drink.

"If I see you around here again, I will have Michail cut your face off." He says, nodding towards the large fellow sitting at the other end of the table.

You get up with your money and walk out of the poker room via the door you came in.

DOUBLE your MONEY you started the game with and UPDATE your Cash on your player Cash sheet.

Turn to 68.

46

—

You head back down the side of the building to the front where the man is still unloading boxes.

Turn to 86.

47

———

As you approach Scarlett's the bouncer outside clocks you. He changes his relaxed stance into one that is more akin to being ready to fight. It is almost as if he's been waiting for you.

You know Leon's in there. You are so close to the satisfaction of killing him. So close to being able to prove to yourself that you aren't a waste of space. You don't care if you die in the process.

But, you need to survive long enough to get to him and right now, this club bouncer is in your way.

He starts to walk towards you as you approach. Your gut instinct tells you he's not even going to talk. He knew you were coming and he's not letting you inside.

You could try and reason with him before he reaches you. Perhaps if you had enough money you could try and pay your way into the club. It may cost a fair bit though to get past this guy.

You have to decide.

If you have £2000 and try and bribe the doorman with it, **Turn to 38.**

If you don't have the cash or choose to fight him, **Turn to 88.**

48

———

Flailing wildly you somehow manage to get your foot into the bouncer's face. A quick kick to his face was enough to make him lose his grip. With both of you on the floor, it didn't take much to move faster than he and deliver the killing blow.

You suddenly realise you are out on the street. You look around but see no one about in the darkness and the pouring rain. You quickly drag his body over to the car park. You don't need to hide him well. Just long enough to give you time to do what you need to do tonight. He's also incredibly heavy.

You move him close to Leon's bike and push the bike somewhere more useful.

Then, enter the club via the front doors. There is no-one else around at the front entrance, and you let yourself inside.

Turn to 59.

49

___

Something went wrong.

You thought you had him. He had taken so many hits. You were covered in blood, and it seemed like it was mostly his. Holding him against the wall by his throat, you could see the life slipping away from him as you looked him in the eye. You didn't see him take the knife. You only felt the cold steel of the blade tear through your skin into your ribs.

The pain made you cry out in agony, and you lost your grip on him instantly. He removed the blade swiftly before you fell backwards and collapsed on the floor.

You open your eyes to feel Leon on top of you. His disfigured face is grinning at you with his sickly torn skin tearing and bleeding with every smile.

With Leon on top of you, he raises both his hands high with the knife gripped between them and reigns down a killing blow.

You block it, arms outstretched under his, but his leverage over you is too powerful. Despite giving every ounce of strength you have left within you, the knife moves closer and closer to your chest.

You panic, realising you cannot stop this.

"NO NO, please….wait, WAIT!" you cry as you feel

the tip of the blade sinking through your skin and into your chest. Hearing your own desperate words out loud turns your stomach, and you feel immense fear riding through your body as you lay here, alone, dying at the hands of this evil human being.

You cannot stop it. The pain and agony of a blade slowly moving deeper and deeper into your chest shocks you to your core. The pain is paralysing, and you lose your strength. From there it is easy for Leon to send the rest of the blade into you. He brings his nose right up to yours. His eyes are the last thing you see as your world turned to darkness.

It was the most horrifying and lonely way to leave this world.

Now you are gone, and Leon will continue to wreak havoc on anything and anyone he wants.

You failed yourself, and you failed Lucy.

50

You choose to open the red door to the kitchen. Upon doing so, you find a tiled room full of silver cooking surfaces and equipment.

Three unshaven, grubby looking men wearing dirty blood-stained aprons are chopping up meat with machetes. They all stop what they are doing when you walk in and turn to face you.

At the back, you also notice what looks like the chef, smoking a cigarette.

He looks across the room at you and speaks to you in an eastern European accent you struggle to place.

"You shouldn't have come here." He says, looking around the kitchen as if bored.

"Kill him".

Without hesitation, the three men armed with machetes bombard you. Swinging their machetes with such venomous force and violence that you can do nothing to protect yourself.

Blades slice deep through your flesh and into your bone as you scream and wail in the sheer agony of being chopped up alive.

No one deserves to die in this way. It should have been

Leon, not you.

You failed her.

51

———

It hurts like a motherfucker, but you pull your hand through the handcuffs breaking your left thumb in the process. You feel the joint break and let out a muffled cry, trying not to attract attention. Thankfully, however, whoever put the cuffs on you failed to realise that with one hand free you could lift the chair and pull the cuffs through.

You are free. You use your right hand to untie the bounds on your feet. It's a little tricky with one hand now out of action, but you manage it.

You stand up and look at your left hand, the locked cuffs still dangling from the wrist of your right hand. You have lost a little skin, but the bone is definitely broken. You won't be able to hold anything in that hand.

You look at the table and notice everything has gone. Leon must have taken it all with him.

Then the door to the room opens. Lazlo walks in. The look of astonishment on his face when he sees you out of your chair is priceless.

You will have to fight him again — this time with a broken thumb and a gash wound to your leg. Everything you have fought for tonight rides on beating him.

Lose -1 ATT before this fight due to your injury.

LAZLO
ATT 5
WND 4

If you win, **Turn to 37.**

If you lose, **Turn to 24.**

52

You try to sneak past Leon from your crouched position, but the moment you move, he clocks you. He runs at you with no thought and pins you against the wall. Both of you are struggling to breathe amid the flames, but this is a fight to the death.

Turn to 42.

53

———

ADD +1 to your SNEAK level.

Being barefooted helps as you leave the room quietly. You carefully make sure the door doesn't slam closed behind you as you leave. Once closed you race down the hallway as quietly as you can, taking a glance over your shoulder as you go through the double doors leaving the hall. The officer hasn't stirred. You made it!

You leave the hallway to find busy corridors full of staff and patients all making their way to different areas of the hospital. It's easy to fit in.

Turn to 62

54

You lose the fight. The first henchman, the bigger of the two, stands over your beaten body. The other is getting up after taking your first hit. The big guy takes your arms and pins your back to his chest, presenting you as a target for the smaller guy.

After getting up and brushing himself down the smaller henchman walks over to you and puts his face right up inside yours.

"This is from Leon," he says as the knife you didn't even see plunges deep into your ribcage. You gasp and cry out at the same time. The pain is unbearable.

You didn't see the second coming either as the cold icy sting comes again and again. You lose count how many times he stabs you. You go into a state of shock. The henchman never takes his eyes off yours the entire time. He wanted to see you suffer. He enjoyed it. His face now splattered in your blood as he smirks at you.

The larger henchman drops you to the ground. You are soaking in the rain, covered in your blood, lying in your front garden.

You hear one of them spit on your lifeless body as they walk off and leave you to die.

As you slip away to the sound of the rain hitting the grass and the thunder overhead, you can smell her perfume. Stronger than ever, riding upon the wind.

"Lucy" is the last thing you say…… as your world goes black.

55

The wind and rain are relentless, and it takes a good 45 minutes to walk into town. It is exhausting, and you feel weaker for making the journey, especially after days of not eating.

Take -1 from your WOUNDS total on your player sheet.

As you make your way towards town, you notice a clock in a kebab shop that is just shutting up for the night. It's one of those cheap plastic clocks with the date on them as well. Wednesday, 01:00 am.

Tuesday night? Lucy died on Saturday night. It's been three days???

The realisation shocks you somewhat, but it makes no difference. You hope Leon is still around. He's a dead man walking.

The area around you begins to build up as you continue walking. More shops and commercial premises the closer you get towards town. You start to cross the road when you are startled by a pair of headlights coming your way from the direction of the town.

You panic when you realise it's a police car, AND IT'S SLOWING DOWN towards you. It's dark and very wet so they may not have seen you, but it'll be odd that someone is out this time of night, and they'll probably be out looking for you. You can't get caught, or it'll all be over.

Turn to 10.

56

———

You enter the bar via the front door. Inside, all the lights are on. A TV sits above the bar showing a football game, and there is music playing in the distance. The whole place is empty. There is no sign of the barman, but you can hear some noise coming from one of the backrooms.

Some police crime scene tape remains although it looks like it has been disturbed as if someone has been trying to peel it off everything. Some of the bar stools seem to be missing, and you notice the bloodstains on the floor. Someone has tried to clear it up but failed miserably.

You become momentarily mesmerised by the thought that this stain is all that remains of Lucy. It's the first time you've seen anything of her since that night.

Choking back the tears you remember lying on the floor with her, covered in her blood. You remember the fear you felt. How paralysed you felt.

You don't feel fearful anymore. You lost your one chance of real happiness when she was taken. There is nothing left here for you. All you care about now is doing the one thing you've always failed at your whole life. Leon has to pay, and you want to see him die beyond anything else. Beyond your self-preservation. You would die to see Leon die.

You only hope that his death will come before yours.

You feel the anger build up inside you again as you decide to head out to the back room to find the barman when he appears holding a mop and a bucket.

He stops in his tracks, mouth open and drops the bucket of water.

"Y-y-y-you" he stutters. "I thought you were dead?".

He looks scared, perhaps mystified.

"I want information," you say.

"Uh, ok, sure. I don't want any trouble."

"Tell me where Leon is."

"I-I can't. I mean, I don't know. He's probably left town by now anyway".

You swiftly move towards the barman and grab his shirt. You pull him towards you over the bar and put your face into his face, aware that he is no longer holding the mop and holding his hands up in surrender.

"TELL ME OR I'LL SMASH YOUR FUCKING FACE IN"

'Ok, listen. I think he's still in town. I can tell you where to find him".

You release him and let him brush himself down. "give me a drink too. "

"Ok……Fuck. Shit man, I'm so sorry. If I knew he was going to do that I'd have……well. It's Leon man. You don't mess with Leon".

"Fuck you, just get me a drink".

"Ok man, be cool yeah, what do you want? Vodka, Whiskey?"

If you choose the Vodka, **Turn to 92.**

If you choose the Whiskey, **Turn to 5.**

———

57

You walk into the shelter of the workshop where the man is pulling the seats out of a car. He is a large man, well built and looks over 6ft tall. A brute wearing grey overalls with a name sewn into the right breast. GREGOR. He sees you enter and stops what he is doing.

"What do you want?" he asks in some accent. Perhaps Russian?

"I'm looking for Leon, where is he?".

"Why do you want to speak to Leon?"

"It's business, where is he"

"Hah," Gregor scoffs. "Leon has no business with you".

At that moment the lifts a large long spanner from his toolbox and begins walking towards you with intent. This man is not going to talk. You must fight.

GREGOR
ATT 4
WND 4

If you win, **Turn to 30.**
If you lose, **Turn to 20.**

58

You get back to the car without seeing another soul and begin the short drive to the seafront pier. You park up as early as you can and walk the rest of the distance.

Driving around in a stolen car is not a smart idea when you want to avoid the police, and it'll be easier to escape on foot if you get seen.

The rain is still lashing down. It never stops.

You can see the pier in the distance. You must be close to Scarlett's.

Turn to 66.

59

———

Upon entering Scarlett's, you are greeted by a vast room. The lighting is low, but several strobe lights and stage lights light it up enough to allow you to see what you need to see. To the right-hand side is a bar. You see the barman minding his own business, polishing glasses. He hasn't noticed you.

To the left is the stage. On stage is a woman in lingerie, swinging on a pole and entertaining a handful of men throwing cash at her.

Straight ahead of you on the far side of the room, you see two men standing outside a closed door, deep in discussion.

One of them is LEON!

You'd recognise that disfigured face from anywhere. Your stomach turns in knots as the hatred you felt since you left the hospital intensifies. You want him to suffer more than he has ever suffered before. You are so close.

He is animatedly talking to another man. A taller man in a blue suit, with an eastern European look about him. Leon slaps the guy around the head as if to express a point and then goes through the door into the next room. The tall man follows and then closes the door behind him.

You head across the room, past the stage and bar. You are walking up to the door. You hesitate for a second and then open the door calmly. You do not want to attract any attention at this stage.

Turn to 7.

60

The man who murdered Lucy stands before you. The man who took away your only chance of real genuine happiness. You have gone through so many trials and tests to get here tonight and suffered pain and sorrow at the hands of this man.

You have surpassed every single hurdle, and every single test thrown at you.

It is time to finish this.

LEON 'THE FACE'
ATT 5
WND 8

If you win, **Turn to 41.**

If you lose, **Turn to 49.**

———

61

You go all-in, and all other players except Eddie fold. Eddie calls your bet.

You lay down your cards face-up on the table, a KD and KH. Eddie looks worried as he lays his cards down in front of you.

A 10S and a 7S. A real weak hand against your pair of Kings. But it isn't over yet.

The cards come down in the middle of the table. 4C, AC, and a 7D. Eddie has a pair of 7's, but it's not enough to beat your Kings. Two more cards to go.

The next card comes down. It's 4D; both players now have two pairs.

Finally, the last card is flipped over.

Your stomach churns as you see it's a 7H.

You cannot believe it! It was almost as if the game was rigged. Eddie beats your two pair Kings and 4's 4's, with a Full House 7's and 4's.

You lose. You probably should have realised this was a rigged game.

Eddie takes your chips while laughing. You gulp at the very idea of taking on six men in a fight.

"Get lost"" he says. "SCRAM!"".

"I can go?"".

Eddie gets up from the table and walks over to the bar. He picks up a whiskey and pours himself a drink.

"I can't be bothered today. I already got your money. But if I see you around here again, I will have Michail cut your face off."" He says, nodding towards the large fellow sitting at the other end of the table.

You get up without your money and walk out of the poker room via the door you came in.

DEDUCT ALL Cash from your Cash on your Player Sheet.

Turn to 68.

62

The hospital is busy tonight with many patients and staff coming and going in some rush. Others are gingerly making their way to different wards. You know you don't have long before someone comes looking for you. You half expect to hear someone shout out at any minute. You need to leave soon.

You purposefully want to avoid the main entrance/exit. If anyone is looking for you, then that's where they'll be waiting. You see a hospital map on the wall and choose to follow a turning into another hallway which should lead towards a rear exit.

The hallway is dead and silent. No patients, no staff.

As you start to move down the hallway, you notice a door, ajar. It looks like a tiny staff cloakroom. There doesn't seem to be anyone inside, but you see a pile of messy clothes hanging out of an open locker. Someone must have been in a rush to get to their shift perhaps.

You're going to look strange running around town in a hospital gown and no belongings. The clothes look like they could fit, but it's hard to tell from the doorway. You'd have to go in and try, but you don't have much time. At any moment, you could be caught. You need to get out of here.

You have a choice to make.

If you enter the room to change into the clothes, **Turn to 77.**

If you ignore the room and continue to reach the rear exit, **Turn to 70.**

63

———

The two shadows notice you and begin to walk quickly towards you. Their body language is obvious. They are not here to talk. You cannot run.

HENCHMAN #1
ATT 3
WND 4

HENCHMAN #2
ATT 4
WND 3

You must fight both men separately.

If you win, **Turn to 84.**

If you lose, **Turn to 54.**

64

———

You gracefully dodge into the bushes on the other side of the road. The rain beating down on the police car windshield probably made it difficult for them to see.

They saw something, though, as they slow down as they roll past the bushes. You hear mechanical car window roll down, and your heart sits in your chest as you stay perfectly still and silent.

The rain continues to punish everything it touches and the police officer is getting wet. He rolls his window back up, and the car continues to move along.

You stay where you are for a few moments to make sure they have gone before you get up and continue your journey.

That was too close!

ADD +1 to your SNEAK level.

You continue to make your way to the bar.

Turn to 71.

65

———

You race from your crouched position and rush past Leon to the door. He doesn't see you until you are closing the door upon him.

You use your body weight and your broken hand to try and stop him from turning the handle, looking at him through the reinforced glass window in the door. His face is sheer panic, and he is screaming in fear.

Your heart is pounding in your chest as you know that at any moment, your damaged hand may not be able to hold the handle. Letting go might allow him to escape. You are so close!

You frantically rummage through the keys you took off Lazlo trying to find the key that looked like it might fit the door. It's hard to do with one hand.

There! You found it! You insert it into the lock and twist. The bolt slides into place, and you let out a sigh of relief. You leave the key lodged in the keyhole and watch Leon from the window.

By now half the room is engulfed in flames, and you begin to hear bottles exploding and flames shooting across the room. Leon's Leon's screams are blood-curdling as he frantically tries to break the window with his fists. The reinforced glass is taking no apparent damage.

A look then appears over Leon's face which you would describe as relief or almost a happiness. He suddenly runs over to the fire escape on the other side of the room, not yet engulfed in flame.

He tries to push the door open, but it won't budge. He tries again, without luck. He begins to cry out again in panic. His last hope taken away from him.

"NO, NOT LIKE THIS!!!!" he screams as he looks at the flames starting to light parts of his clothing.

It must be so hot in there. You can no longer stand close to the door; the heat must be unbearable inside.

Desperately Leon steps back and takes a run-up to the fire escape. He launches his entire body at it in a bid to make it move. The door remains closed.

Of course, he won't be able to open it the whole time his bike is propped up against it.

Before you came in through the front door of the club, you placed his motorbike against the door, using his security chain and the nearby dumpsters for added effect. It'll take an army to break that door open.

Leon looks at you, in agony, knowing what you have done. The flames are now riding up his trousers and almost reaching his waist.
He looks at you with a shocked stare, you recognise very well.

"For Lucy," you say to him, as you leave the room back into the hallway.

You make your way back into the main club room. The room is usually smoky, and it seems no one has noticed that the rear half of the building is now on fire. Punters are still throwing money at the girl on stage, and the barman is busy chatting to a guy who has had too much to drink.

As you walk through the room, the fire alarm triggers. Half clothed dancers and miserable old punters scurry to the front door with you as you leave through the front entrance.

You flood out into the car park, amid a panic-stricken and confused crowd.

Suddenly an explosion rips through the back of the club, sending flames billowing out from the rear exit. The crowd flinch in shock. Leon's bike is sent across the other side of the alleyway as the fire exit door is blown open. Flames are pouring out from the room you were just inside.

The room is entirely engulfed in flame. Amid the chaos inside, you can no longer hear Leon's screams.

As the various fire engines begin to arrive at the scene, you notice the rain has finally stopped. You walk away, nursing your leg and hand into the dark early morning of the next day unnoticed amid the chaos you leave behind.

You may not have been able to help her. She may no

longer be here. But for once in your sorry life, you've done the one thing you've never had the courage to do.

Stand up and fight. And you'll fight now until the end of your days.

Turn to 100.

66

——

You have no idea what time it must be, but it has to be late.

This has been a long night. Your determination has seen you through. The hate and anger you're feeling are consuming you. You want to find him. Ask him why. Then make him feel pain.

All your paths have led you to this place. A bright reddy/pink neon sign with 'Scarlett's' sits atop the entrance of a club with a neon outline of a pair of lips.

There's no queue to get in. It looks quiet inside. Just a bouncer, standing in the doorway, under the overhang to keep out of the rain as best he can. He hasn't seen you.

The club sits on the corner of two intersecting roads as it joins the seafront. Next to the club sits a car park. It is mostly empty but for four or five cars and a Harley Davidson motorcycle close to a rear entrance.

You instantly recognise it as the same Harley you saw Leon driving away on from the bar that night. Your stomach turns in knots before a new rage fills you once again.

He's here. Leon is inside.

You have two choices.

Will you head to the front of the club and go in via the front entrance, somehow dealing with the bouncer? If so, **Turn to 47.**

Or will you go in via the rear door and try to find Leon this way? If so, **Turn to 80.**

———

67

In diving towards you from a distance, you manage to dodge his advance and pivot around behind him.

The blow to the head you gave him put the rest of the fight in your favour. It may have been pure luck; it certainly wasn't skill. But you won.

You didn't want him to get back up, so you finished him off in style.

During the attack it looked as if he was reaching for something from his belt. You turn his now lifeless body over to find a knife holster containing a knife.

You instantly recognise it. Lucy's knife. The one that Leon used to kill her.

You take it.

REPLACE whatever you are carrying with this knife and add +3 ATTACK to your attacks.

You shut the fire door and move out into the next room. You know someone out there is probably waiting for you.

As you move inside, however, you find three doors. All closed.

One door is green, with no signs on it at all.

The other is red and is labelled KITCHEN.

The third door is blue and is labelled OFFICE.

Lazlo called out before the struggle. It's likely that someone heard. It's also highly likely that Leon could be behind one of these doors.

Which one will you choose to enter?

If you choose the green door with no markings, **Turn to 16.**

If you choose the red door marked KITCHEN, **Turn to 50.**

If you choose the blue door marked OFFICE, **Turn to 75.**

68

———

You get out of the poker house fast and step back out into the rain. This was a dead-end lead, and you've wasted plenty of time.

It's time to get back on track and find Leon.

By now he'll probably know you're looking for him.

You get back to the car without seeing another soul and begin the short drive to the seafront pier. You park up as early as you can and walk the rest of the distance. Driving around in a stolen car is not a smart idea when you want to avoid the police, and it'll be easier to escape on foot if you get seen.

The rain is still lashing down. It never stops.

You can see the pier in the distance. You must be close to Scarlett's.

Turn to 66.

69

———

You weren't fast enough in the fight. Lazlo has some real fighting experience, unlike you. He blocks most of your swings and lands some real hits on you. Before you realise what's happening, he's holding a knife.

You recognise the knife, but your brain doesn't have a chance to comprehend that it's the knife that Leon used to kill Lucy.

A searing pain screams up your leg as you look down to see the blade being removed from your leg. Warm blood begins to pour out of the wound. As your attention remains focused on the injury Lazlo stabs you in the chest with almost military precision.

The blade remains stuck between your rib cage, however, and Lazlo struggles to pull it back out. You don't get to see what happens next. The room goes black, and your fight is over.

You lost, and you failed her....again.

70

You scurry down the hallway and see the exit. Careful not to run and attract attention to yourself. It is a fire escape that can only be opened from the inside. You hear raised voices coming from behind you.

Hitting the bar to the fire door hard with both hands, the heavy door swings open to the outside world.

It's dark, cold, howling a gale and rain is lashing down. You have no idea what time it is other than it is night.

There's no one around the back here. The odd staff member is moving trolleys or delivering supplies, trying to get out of the rain. Wrapped up in their own problems, no one takes any notice of you as you walk out into the dark wet night.

It's time to find Leon.

Turn to 23.

—

71

You eventually arrive at the bar. The 'AfterDark'. A seedy grubby late-night bar that neither of you would usually be anywhere near. For some reason, she recognised it from her past. She said she couldn't put her finger on when she had been there, but the smile on her face told you she remembered.

You'd only been in there 20 minutes when you had left to go to the bathroom. That's when it all kicked off. You heard the motorcycle pull up and the voices in the bar. You heard people leave before other voices became raised. You thought you heard screaming and shouting. It sounded like Lucy. That's when you came out and found her and Leon screaming at each other.

Did she know Leon? Did she know him from her past? The barman knew him, that's for sure. You recall the moment the barman held her down onto her seat. He shouldn't have put his hands on her.

The anger snaps you out of the memory, and you look up at the bar again. It seems open although you cannot see anyone inside. You notice a side passage which appears to lead to a back door.

If you go in via the front door, **Turn to 56.**

If you go in via the back door, **Turn to 79.**

72

You don't know how you managed to lose to a guy already on the floor and, but you did it. He even managed to knock you out.

Now you've come to, and you're tied up and bound by your hands and feet. He's done a great job of it too. The smell is revolting, and you deduce that you're possibly inside a dumpster bin. Tied up in polythene sheeting, you cannot see a thing. You try to shout, but there is something in your mouth — a gag ball of some kind.

You slip in and out of consciousness, having no idea how much time has passed. You come around a little later to the sounds of beeping and a loud truck engine.

You are still disorientated and trying to work out what is going on when the whole dumpster becomes weightless. You are in the air.

Before you can do anything, your whole world turns upside down, literally, as you come falling out of the dumpster. You can't see much wrapped inside some black polythene, but moments later you let out a blood-curdling scream in sheer agony as the press of the dumpster truck comes down on top of you, crushing your body. You feel the immense pressure crush your skull as you die.

73

———

You took the Barman's keys earlier. The car key with the VW logo on it made it easy to find. It was also the only one outside the bar.

A short drive across town. It didn't take long to find — a sorry-looking building on an industrial estate right next to the old cinema. Despite moving here two years ago, you've never been down this part of town.

You decide to pull up a few buildings short of the garage and walk down. It's dark and once again the lighting down here is inadequate. Great for keeping a low profile however as you stick to the shadows as much as you can.

As you approach the garage, you can see the light is switched on coming from the upper floor. It looks like the office is up there, and the body shop is down on the ground floor. As you approach near, you can hear some noise.

You crouch down and use the darkness as cover. As you get closer, you can see someone in a black coat unloading boxes from a parked up truck and taking them into the garage. He seems to be alone. It doesn't look like Leon. Too tall and skinny. You see cigarette smoke billow from his face against the security light that lights up the front entrance of the garage. He unloads the boxes one by one in the relentless rain and places them inside the garage next to another parked car. He's muttering to himself and seems unhappy. He is probably frustrated at being out in this rain.

You creep up closer, wanting to get a good look before you blow your cover.

The parked car seems to have been stripped down, and bags of white powder have been taped onto the interior frames of the vehicle — drugs of some kind. Perhaps a smugglers run or something.

You watch the guy taking the packets out of the box and taping them to the inside of the car.

Now closer to the building, you also see some stairs leading up the side of the building to what looks like offices upstairs. You can see a light on up there.

There's also a side path leading around the back of the building which you could investigate and get a full picture of what's going on here. You don't want to walk into a building full of thugs and get the shit beaten out of you.

You have a choice to make.

If you head around the back to see what you can find, **Turn to 25.**

If you talk to the guy out the front unloading boxes, **Turn to 86.**

If instead, you decide to creep up the stairs to the **offices, Turn to 95.**

You decide to open the blue door to the office.

Upon doing so, you immediately notice someone is inside. Cigarette smoke fills the messy, paper-strewn office. A simple desk covered in paperwork sits in the middle of the room, with just enough space to walk either side of it. There are no windows, but CCTV monitors line the left walls.

Small mini-screens are showing a kitchen with people cooking. Another shows the main stage and another showing the entrance as well.

You notice the final monitor fixated on Lazlo's body and realise someone has been watching you the whole time.

Behind the desk facing you sits Leon. He is laying back in his chair, feet up on the table, smoking a cigar. He seems extremely calm.

"Take a seat, let's talk" he offers, calmly before taking another drag of his cigar.

You choose to remain standing at the doorway. It is the only way out of the room.

"I was surprised how easily you took down my best guy. Lazlo was ex-military. I mean, you were lucky, but sheesh, I never expected him to go down so easy".

You remain silent.

"You're a quiet one. Fair enough. I'm a talker".

He looks at you, frustrated at your lack of conversation.

"Why," you ask. "Why did you do it?"

Leon smirks and then slowly gets up from his desk.

"My friend, I know that you've taken a blow to the head. But are you that dense?"

"You knew her?"

Leon smiles. "It was a bit more than that," he says, laughing.

"What did she ever do to you?" you ask.

Leon explodes from his calm demeanour into a violent rage. "WHAT DID SHE FUCKING DO????". He points to his disfigured burned face. Now given the time to study his face, you can see where it looks as if he suffered a terrible burn. Skin looks like it has melted and been fused back as best it could be. The flesh still looks grossly sore, and you can see areas where it is even tearing apart whenever he uses his facial muscles. You're sure the pain would have been unbearable.

"THIS! THIS is what she did to me."

You look at him in disbelief. The woman you know

would never have inflicted such an injury on someone for no reason. You wonder what he must have done for her to inflict that level of pain on someone. She was never the violent type.

"What did you do to her?"

Leon's demeanour violently flips from calm to rage and back to calm. It is as if he has no control.

"Ok, ok. I may have been a bit rough with her." He says smiling with a jokey tone, then erupting again into a rage "But that is NO fucking excuse for what she did. She burned me and made me suffer a pain no man should suffer!"

"I should have killed her long ago." He adds, now calm again, but building into yet another eruption. "She should never have come back. Fancy meeting her in the bar that night? Who did she think she was, coming back to MY TOWN!!!!, after what she did".

You look at him, envisaging what you are going to do to him. You feel no sorrow for his story.

You reach over the desk and pull Leon over it with an almost superhuman strength that you never knew you had. You lean in, but Leon violently throws his head towards you and connects. You take the full force of his headbutt in the face, knocking you back. By the time you get yourself back up on your feet, Leon has leapt over the desk and is coming towards you.

You must fight Leon, but you are on the back foot.

DEDUCT -1 ATTACK from your score before you begin the fight.

Turn to 60.

76

You weren't fast enough in the fight. Lazlo has some real fighting experience, unlike you. He blocks most of your swings and lands some real hits on you. Before you realise what's happening, he's holding a knife.

You recognise the knife, but your brain doesn't have a chance to comprehend that it's the knife that Leon used to kill Lucy.

A searing pain screams up your leg as you look down to see Lazlo has cut your leg. Warm blood begins to pour out of the wound. As your attention is focused on the injury, Lazlo hits you square in the face with his fist.

Turn to 17.

—

77

You enter the room and notice you were right. There is no one there. But you don't have much time.

You begin changing your clothes and breathe a sigh of relief as you realise the clothes fit fine. A little baggy, but that's not a problem.

Subconsciously you also begin to rummage through the locker to see if there is anything else of use. To your surprise, you find a thin wad of cash. You quickly count it up to find you are holding $290.

You also notice a toolbox on the ground with a Hammer sticking out of it. You may need a weapon if you get into trouble. Leon will not be easy to kill.

It is your choice.

If you decide to take the HAMMER, add it to your WEAPONS list on your player sheet and ADD +1 to your ATTACK score.

If you also decide to take the $290, ADD it to the CASH section on your player sheet. You can choose to take none of it, some of it, or all of it. The amount you take is entirely up to you and your conscience.

Once done, **Turn to 70**

78

Your heart skips a beat in fear as your logical brain tells you no one should be at your home at this hour.

The two figures are dressed in black clothing and coats. They are not policemen.

They are silent as if waiting. Probably for you. But they haven't yet seen you.

If you choose to fight them, **Turn to 63.**

If instead, you choose to try and SNEAK past them, **Turn to 11.**

79

——

You decide to enter the bar using the back door.

Inside it is dark, but you can hear someone moving around. As you round the corner, you find the barman in a toilet room wringing blood out from a mop. He is dressed in an apron.

"What the…." The barman is startled by your sudden entrance. He recognises you from that night and is visibly shaken to see you here. He goes to reach for something in his pocket. A phone maybe.

You don't give him a chance.

You smack him in the face, hard, busting his nose open.

He falls back, still conscious, blood pouring down his face.

"Where's Leon" you demand.

"Haha, not fucking here! He's going to kill you, man. You know this is his joint right? He's gonna kill you for this".

The guy isn't talking, but he will. He knows where Leon is; it's just going to take a bit of work to find out.

You must fight him.

BARMAN
ATT 3
WND 3

If you win, **Turn to 29.**

If you lose, **Turn to 72.**

80

You manage to open the fire escape from the outside. It was left slightly ajar. Just enough to get your fingers in to pull it open.

As you enter the building, you find yourself in what seems to be a tiled store room filled with boxes of liquor and a massive supply of Vodka. Presumably for the clubs bar perhaps.

On the right is an empty table, to the left is a chair in the far corner of the room. Opposite you is a slightly open door with a reinforced window.

You hear voices.

Just then, the door opens further, and a figure fills the doorway. A tall man, in a navy suit. He has an eastern European look about him.

You have never seen this man before, but he seems to know who you are or at least why you are there.

"HE'S HERE!" he shouts back to whomever he was speaking before he entered.

He then leaps towards you; you must fight him.

Turn to 6.

81

———

You decide that bribing this guy was probably never going to work anyway.

A sudden realisation comes across the doorman's eyes, which then suddenly turns to anger.

He comes towards you armed with nothing, but he doesn't need a weapon. His monstrous figure looks like it could pummel you into the very carpet you stand on.

You decide the area is too close-quartered to fight him, so you run down the narrow hallway back to the front door.

You frantically try to open the door latch panicking as you struggle with your wet hands.

You can hear his footsteps running towards you down the hall.

You twist, and it opens, as you jump outside into the pouring rain before turning to face him as he steps out behind you.

"I'm going to enjoy this" he says as he walks towards you.

You must fight.

DOORMAN
ATT 4
WND 4

If you lose, **Turn to 87.**

If you win, **Turn to 39.**

82

———

You don't win. You can't. Not against this guy.

You're not fast enough in the fight. Lazlo has some real fighting experience, unlike you. He blocks most of your swings and lands some real hits on you. Before you realise what's happening, he's holding a knife.

You recognise the knife, but your brain doesn't have a chance to comprehend that it's the knife that Leon used to kill Lucy.

A searing pain screams up your leg as you look down to see Lazlo has cut your leg. Warm blood begins to pour out of the wound. As your attention is focused on the injury, Lazlo hits you square in the face with his fist.

Turn to 17.

83

———

Your bus journey home was uneventful. The whole bus was empty. You spent most of the time thinking about Lucy and how you'll kill Leon when you find him. You ring the bell as you notice the bus approaching the stop nearest your home and shout at the driver through the wind and rain to confirm the day and time as you step off.

"Day?" he scoffs, raising his voice to be heard. "It's Tuesday night. 1 am, so technically Wednesday" he replies before closing the bus doors smiling away to himself in disbelief and driving off.

Tuesday night? Lucy died on Saturday night. It's been three days???

The realisation shocks you somewhat, but it makes no difference. You hope Leon is still around. He's a dead man walking.

The roads are quiet, especially as you reach your neighbourhood. But the wind and rain are loud, and it's just started to thunder.

As you eventually approach your house, it's dark. Lucy always used to complain about the lack of streetlights down your road. She was planning to run a campaign with the local council about it.

You open the walkway gate leading up to the front

door of your home. You are now in the privacy of your property. The 20ft high tall fern trees that line the front garden are swaying violently in the wind and rain. Your head is down as you focus on getting to your front door. Maybe that's why you missed them…..

Two shadows. Standing by the front door.

Turn to 78.

After dealing with those two scumbags, you head around to the back door.

It's still locked, so you use the spare key which you've always kept under a dragon statue Lucy bought for the back garden.

Careful not to switch any lights on in case someone else is watching the house you grab your rucksack. You fill it with some food from the kitchen. You're incredibly hungry and feeling a little weak. You'll eat this stuff once you've left the house. You need to get away from here fast.

ADD +1 to your WOUND to reflect added strength.

In the downstairs games room, you see your pride and joy. A Wade Boggs autographed baseball bat. Lucy bought it for your birthday; it must've cost thousands. You take a moment to think about that awesome day when a noise from outside the front door startles you.

You have no time for memories. You must get what you need and get out quick before you're noticed.

You also remember the $1000 cash you have stashed under the floorboard in that room. It would be very easy to take. Lucy always said she wanted it there in the case of emergencies. Looks like she was right, again.

You can take the BASEBALL BAT the $1000 or both.

If you decide to take the BASEBALL BAT, add it to your WEAPONS list on your player sheet removing any other items you may be carrying already along with their bonuses, and then ADD +2 to your ATTACK score.

If you also decide to take the $1000, add it to the MONEY section on your player sheet. You can choose to take none of it, some of it, or all of it. The amount you take is entirely up to you.

Now it's time to get out of here. It's a 30-minute walk to the bar where Lucy died. You'll start there.

Turn to 71.

85

You try to dive for cover, but the two men see you.

"Oh, hey. Sorry" says the taller one. Are you a member?

"Of course he's a fucking member you twat, why else would he be standing here waiting to get in?" says the shorter of the two men. Both wrestling to put on their coats. The taller one looks out in the rain. "Fuck, it's still raining".

He then turns to you.

"Eddies got it rigged tonight, so play defensive".

The shorter one scoffs. "He still got all your money thought, didn't he?".

"Fuck you I'm a good player" argues the taller man.

They both run off into the night, coats raised above their heads in a weak attempt to shield themselves from the rain.

You walk through the door into the building and close it behind you.

Turn to 35.

———

86

You clear your throat. The tall man in the black coat drops the box he's carrying and turns around to face you.

"WHO'S THERE?" he says in alarm.

"Hey," you say, stepping forward into the light. "I'm looking for Leon, have you seen him?".

The guy says nothing for a moment. You're about to fill the awkward silence when he takes a step closer, leans in and asks "Hey, are you the guy?".

"The guy?" you ask, uncertain of what he means.

"Yeah, the guy with the dead wife," he says, looking over his shoulder and being sure to keep his voice down.

The laid-back nature of how he addressed Lucy pisses you off. You envisage beating this guys head in just for saying those words.

You don't realise it, lost in your anger, but your eyes are looking through your eyebrows. Covered in blood, standing in the rain, you probably look a little psychopathic. "where the fuck is Leon?" you repeat. The guy takes a step closer, once again taking a look over his shoulder to check no one is listening.

"Hey man, chill. Listen, I'm going to help you. Leon's not here. But I know where he is tonight."

"Where"? You ask.

The guy lowers his voice more, but loud enough that you can hear over the rain.

"He's at Scarlett's. It's a strip joint down at the seafront opposite the pier. It's closed, but it's open if you catch me. Police down here let him do what he wants. He owns the place. He'll be down there all night. Always is."

"I was told he was inside," you say, pointing at the garage.

"Nah man, you don't want to go in there. Listen, I promise you, he's not here. I know he's at Scarlett's tonight. Trust me".

"Why do you want to help me?" you ask, surprised at the apparent level of treason being committed by one of Leon's men.

"Dude, fuck Leon. He controls everything and everyone. I'm sick of it. He does what he wants and never pays for it. Last week he smacked my girl around the face for nothing but his temper. She's got a broken fucking nose. There's nothing I can do about it if I want to live. The sooner he gets a kicking, the better. But man let me tell you, if you mess with him, make sure you finish the job. You don't want a man like Leon chasing you. You'll be running for a lifetime."

You like this kid. Either he's a fantastic liar, or he's telling the truth. His words, emotions and expressions seem genuine.

"Thanks for the advice" you say, as you turn and walk off back to your car.

Turn to 66.

87

It really was the worst idea you've ever had. Trying to fight this guy was never going to work.

You realise this when he is dragging your half unconscious and limp body in the rain across the floor with one arm. He drags you across the cobbled street over to the curb and makes you bite it before taking a step back.

"Leon sends his love," he says before stamping on the back of you're head.

You die as your skull is crushed and your face tears open against the curb. Bits of your teeth shattering across the cobbles.

This was a bad idea.

88

The bouncer's immense strength enables him to lift you off the ground by your throat. His grip is strangling you. You will need to get free and fight this guy to get into the club and face Leon. And you'll need to do it quickly.

SCARLETT'S BOUNCER
ATT 4
WND 3

If you lose, **Turn to 15.**

If you win, **Turn to 48.**

89

———

ADD +1 to your SNEAK score.

The wind, rain, thunder and darkness make it easy to sneak past the two shadows by your front door. Leon must have sent them.

It's bad news if he knows where you live and must know you're out of the hospital to have sent men to your home. That means the police are probably on the lookout for you too.

You'll have to be quiet inside to not tip them off that you're home.

You enter through the backdoor. It's still locked, so you use the spare key which you've always kept under a dragon statue Lucy bought for the back garden.

Careful not to switch any lights on you enter the house and grab your rucksack. You fill it with some food from the kitchen. You're incredibly hungry and feeling a little weak. You'll eat this stuff once you've left the house. You need to get away from here fast.

ADD +1 to your WOUND to reflect added strength.

You hear movement again at the front door. You're out of time. You've got to get out of here before Leon's men catch you. It's a 30-minute walk to the bar where Lucy died. You'll start there.

Turn to 71.

90

You must fight the Barman

BARMAN
ATT 3
WND 3

If you win, **Turn to 29.**

If you lose, **Turn to 72.**

91

___

ADD +1 to your SNEAK level.

With a silent roll of your body against the wall you swiftly move into the shop next door which has, fortunately, has a concealed alcove entrance, hoping that who is coming doesn't see you.

They unclick the door from the inside and two men, both in long coats step outside. "Fuck, it's still pissing it down," the shorter one says to the other. "Come on, I'm starving, fuck this place," says the taller of the two.

"You're just pissed he took all your money again" the smaller one laughs. They walk off grumbling, unaware of you hiding behind them.

Taking a massive risk to leap to the door as fast and as quietly as you can, while both men are so very close to you, you manage to stop the door before it swings shut with your hand. Superb effort.

You take one last look at the men to ensure they have not heard you, but they are both now running for cover, coats over their heads, trying to get out of the rain. Quickly entering the building and close the door behind you.

Turn to 35.

92

——

"Vodka," you tell the barman.

He looks a little shifty, but you put it down to nerves. He takes a bottle from under the counter and pours you two long shots, spilling some on the bar. He then pushes it over to you.

You grab the first shot and down it instantly, and then the second one. "Again".

He repeats the process, as do you, necking down both shots instantly.

The alcohol burns your throat, and you can feel it slide down your chest.

The barman begins to look calmer all of a sudden, and you feel the room starting to change. It starts to get hot. Incredibly hot. You feel yourself starting to sweat as your throat begins to burn to the point of pain.

"You know, I never liked Leon. He's dirty work, but you never cross that guy. She should never have come back here. You both had it coming" the barman says, as you lose your balance and fall on your ass.

You look up at the barman in disbelief, but you're in too much pain to even comprehend his words.

You start to scream as it feels like your eyes are bulging

from their sockets. They ARE bulging from their sockets! You lose your sight as what feels like molten lava flowing down your throat causes you to lose the ability to breathe. Your chest is on fire, and your stomach cramps in intense pain like you have never felt before as you drop sideways to the floor.

"Leon called just before you got here, said you might drop by." The barman now sounds calmer than ever. Maybe the nervousness was all an act to make you feel in control.

You can't see anything. Your face and nostrils feel like they have melted off. You try to breathe, but you suffocate and die a quick but incredibly painful death.

You have failed Lucy again.

The Vodka was perhaps the wrong choice.

93

You run to dart behind the bushes on the other side of the road, but the entire street illuminates in blue light as the police car lights you up and begins to accelerate towards you.

You've been found.

You give up on the bushes and head down an alleyway between two shops. You have no idea where the alley leads. You hear the sound of raised voices and footsteps running down the alleyway after you.

As you emerge from the alleyway, your heart sinks into your stomach as you see a complete dead-end of a closed shop and dumpster bins. Other than hiding in the containers, there is nowhere for you to go. And they'll look in the containers for sure.

Before you can even turn around to face them to surrender you're thrown to the ground by a police officer who pins you down while his partner radios in for backup.

He cuffs you before you know what's hit you and they both lead you back to the police car.

You think about trying to escape and begin to make a run for it, but they were expecting that. A taser gun fires, sending electrical shocks around your body as you fall to the floor in agony.

They throw you into the back of the car from which you cannot escape.

This is the end of the road for you. You failed Lucy again.

94

—

On your next hand you are dealt KD/AD.

If you go all in here, **Turn to 45.**

If you play another hand, **Turn to 26.**

95

——

You head down the side path of the building and reach the bottom of the stairs. Looking up, you see the light in the office is on. It would seem someone might be up there.

You try to tread quietly but give up. The sound of your shoes on the metal steps is too loud to mask. They'll know someone is coming, but they won't expect 'you'.

You walk into the room without pause. It's a cold, dimly lit room filled with cigarette smoke. A middle-aged guy in a shirt and jeans is sitting at the desk intensely looking at some paperwork and punching numbers into a calculator. It's not Leon.

"Get back to work Jay, stop slacking off," he says without looking up at you.

"I'm not Jay" you answer, closing the door of the office behind you and putting your back against the wall nearby. You don't want someone walking in behind you without you knowing, although you'll hear their footsteps well enough. You also don't want to alert anyone else in case things get messy.

"Who the fuck are you?" The man demands with an authoritative but shaky voice. He leaps out of his chair and stands ready as if he is not sure what to expect.

"I'm here to speak to Leon". You answer. "Where is

he?"

"He's not here for fuck's sake. He's never here.".

You notice the guy subtly reaching for a mobile phone on the desk.

You leap forward and grab the phone, tossing it aside across the room, then grab him by his shift and throw him backwards. The man panics and stumbles back into his chair.

"For fuck's sake. Look, he's not here."

"Then where is he?"

The man hesitates for a moment before responding. "The poker house. He's playing cards tonight at the poker house. He's always there".

"Where is this poker house?" you demand, standing over the worried weasel of a man.

"It's down in the old town. They'll be closed, but he's always there after hours. He owns the place".

"He seems to own a lot of places around here".

"Who Leon?" the man scoffs. "Leon owns everything and every one man. You're playing with fire."

You reach in and grab the guys shirt, smacking him in the face. He's out, cold. At least for a minute.

You walk out, having the information you need. There

is no need to really hurt the guy. Sure, he's bound to tip Leon off the moment you leave. But you don't care. Let him know what's coming.

As you walk down the steps from the office you have a chance to speak to the guy loading boxes, or you can head straight to the poker house.

If you speak to the guy loading boxes at the front of the garage, **Turn to 14.**

If you get back in the car and head to the Poker House, **Turn to 13.**

100

———

Congratulations

You have killed Leon and changed lives forever, including your own. Where you end up next will be another adventure of its own.

Dear Reader, thank you for playing. I sincerely hope you enjoyed the gamebook. I, like many other people from my generation, grew up with the choose your own ending style books and it has always been a life goal of mine to write one.

 After writing this one, I feel like I have developed a bug for it. So there may be more in the future.

If you enjoyed this book, tell others about it. It was written for fans of the genre by a fan of the genre. So I hope you'll do me a favour and pass the word on.

My wholehearted thanks.

 Chris Chillingworth

CONTACT THE AUTHOR

———

Chris Chillingworth built himself a small wood cabin with a log fire in Kent, England and resides there with his partner, children and his collection of modern board games and 80's gamebooks.

A keen poker player, stock market investor and whiskey drinker, you will often find him in his cabin, writing or immersing himself amongst the things he loves doing.

If you'd like to get in touch, you can write to him at

chris@chrischillingworth.com